The

OWL

and the

PUSSY-CAT

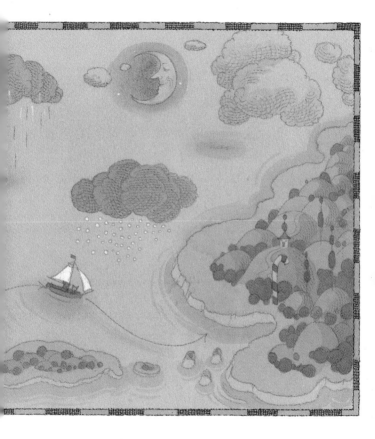

For Emma

THE OWL AND THE PUSSY-CAT
A RED FOX BOOK 0 55 254882 0

First published in Great Britain in 1995 by Doubleday,
an imprint of Random House Children's Books

First Red Fox Mini Treasures edition published 2002

3 5 7 9 10 8 6 4

Copyright © Ian Beck 1995

The right of Ian Beck to be identified as the author and illustrator of this work has
been asserted in accordance with the Copyright, Designs and Patents Act 1988

Red Fox Books are published by Random House Children's Books,
61-63 Uxbridge Road, London W5 5SA,
a division of The Random House Group Ltd,
in Australia by Random House Australia (Pty) Ltd,
20 Alfred Street, Milsons Point, Sydney, NSW 2061, Australia,
in New Zealand by Random House New Zealand Ltd,
18 Poland Road, Glenfield, Auckland 10, New Zealand,
and in South Africa by Random House (Pty) Ltd,
Endulini, 5A Jubilee Road, Parktown 2193, South Africa

THE RANDOM HOUSE GROUP Limited Reg. No. 954009

www.kidsatrandomhouse.co.uk

A CIP catalogue record for this book is available from the British Library.

Printed and bound in Singapore

The
OWL
and the
PUSSY-CAT

EDWARD LEAR

ILLUSTRATED BY
IAN BECK

Mini Treasures

RED FOX

The Owl and the Pussy-cat went to sea

In a beautiful pea-green boat,

They took some honey,

and plenty of money,

Wrapped up in a five-pound note.

The Owl looked up to the stars above,
And sang to a small guitar,

"O lovely Pussy! O Pussy my love,
What a beautiful Pussy you are,
    You are, You are!
        What a beautiful Pussy you are!"

Pussy said to the Owl, "You elegant fowl!
How charmingly sweet you sing!

O let us be married! Too long we have tarried:
But what shall we do for a ring?"

They sailed away, for a year and a day

To the land where the Bong-tree grows

And there in a wood a Piggy-wig stood

With a ring at the end of his nose,
His nose,
His nose,
With a ring at the end of his nose.

"Dear Pig, are you willing to sell for one shilling

Your ring?" Said the Piggy, "I will."

So they took it away, and were married next day

By the Turkey who lives on the hill.

They dined on mince,

and slices of quince,

Which they ate with a runcible spoon;

And hand in hand, on the edge of the sand,

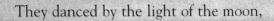
They danced by the light of the moon,

The moon,
The moon,

They danced by the light of the moon.

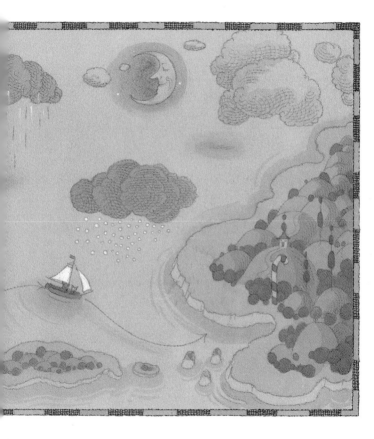